JEREMY THE BIBLE BOOKWORM

TELLS THE STORY OF

NOAH'S ARK

Written by **Roberta Letwenko**

Illustrated by **Edward Letwenko**

Regina Press New York

Jeremy sat at the window watching the raindrops splashing into puddles on the ground. It had been raining for three days. Jeremy missed playing outside with his friends, and had run out of ideas for games to play indoors.

"Maybe Mom will play a game with me," Jeremy thought. He ran to the kitchen. Uncle Beau was just coming in, stomping the wet from his feet and clothes.

"Oh, my," said Uncle Beau, laughing. "I don't believe old Noah himself saw more water than this. It's a good day for some hot clover tea with honey to get rid of the chill."

Jeremy's mother took Uncle Beau's hat and put the kettle on for tea. "Noah?" she asked. "Isn't he from one of those Bible stories you read to Jeremy?"

"That's right," said Beau. "Now that story tells about a <u>real</u> rainstorm — much worse than this one." Uncle Beau gave Jeremy a wink.

As the three of them sat together and sipped their tea, they talked about the terrible rain that lasted forty days and nights. Suddenly a small ray of sun shone through the window and sparkled on the table.

"Well, look at that," Beau said. "It looks like we might have a sunny day after all."

"Hooray!" cried Jeremy. "I'm going outside." Jeremy's mother buttoned him into his rain clothes and out he ran.

The ladybug children were already outside, splashing in the puddles. Jennie Bee was making mud pies with the thick clay-like mud.

Jeremy's friend Basil was watching small leaves and twigs
float by on a large stream of water created by the rain.

"Hey," Jeremy called to Jennie. "Basil's found a river. Come
and see."

Jennie Bee ran to the stream where Jeremy and Basil stood.
"That water is moving pretty fast," said Jennie.

"I'll bet it's really deep too," said Basil.

"You know," said Jeremy, "Uncle Beau and I were just talking about a story from God's book. It was about a man named Noah who built a boat to ride on the water during a flood. Maybe we could build a boat and ride down this river."

"Wow! Wouldn't that be exciting?" said Jennie. "Let's try it."

Basil agreed and the three friends began gathering twigs and leaves to make their boat.

"Jeremy," asked Basil. "How did Noah know there was going to be a flood?"

"Well, according to the Bible, God told him." said Jeremy. "One day God looked at the world and felt very sad. God had made people for love, but they had learned to fight and hate. They lied and cheated and hurt one another. So God decided to send a great rain to flood the earth and wash it clean and beautiful again — the way it was in the beginning."

"Is that where Noah comes in?" Basil asked.

Jeremy nodded. "God saw that Noah was a good man. He told Noah to build an ark — that's a large boat. God said the ark would protect Noah and his family and all the animals."

"Animals?" asked Jennie. "What animals?"

"God told Noah to take two of every kind of animal on earth into the ark — every beast, bird, and creeping thing. God wanted to protect them too," Jeremy explained. "And he told Noah to take enough food along to feed everyone."

"No wonder the ark had to be so big," Basil said.

"Right," said Jeremy. "God told Noah exactly how long and how wide the ark should be. God said it should stand three stories high. Then God told Noah to cover the ark with pitch inside and out to keep it dry."

"Pitch must be something like that sticky clay I was using for mud pies," Jennie said. "Maybe we should fill the holes in our boat with it to keep it from leaking."

The little raft began to take shape as the three friends scurried about binding the twigs together with long strands of prairie grass. They plugged up holes with clay and small leaves.

As they worked, Jeremy continued his story. "Noah and his family followed all of God's directions. They put a window in the roof of the ark and a big door on the side. Inside they made separate rooms for the people, animals, and food. When the ark was finished, it looked just the way God had described it. Noah's boat was ready."

"Our boat is ready too," said Basil proudly. "Let's begin our adventure."

The little group was excited as they pushed their raft into the water.

"Look," said Jennie. "I brought some snacks for our journey. We'll have food, just like Noah."

They began floating slowly down the small stream. The little boat curved this way and that, around small plants and rocks.

"We fit just perfectly on our boat," said Jennie. "I'm sure glad we didn't have to take along all those animals."

"Say," said Basil, "how did Noah get all those animals together to put them on the ark?" "Noah worried about that too," answered Jeremy

"When the ark was finished, the wild creatures came out of the forest and the tame ones came in from the valley. They came by twos, like a parade, and went up the ramp into the ark. I guess God spoke to them too.

"Inside the ark, Noah's sons, Shem, Ham, and Japhet guided the animals into stalls and pens.

"When everyone was inside, Noah and his family waited for seven days. Then one day they heard the splash and splatter of the rain hitting the roof of the ark. It rained harder and harder. The thunder crashed and the wind roared. Lightning flashed across the sky. But they were not afraid. They knew that God would protect them.

"The ark rode up and down on the giant waves. For forty days and forty nights, the rain fell. The whole earth was covered with water."

Suddenly Jennie cried out, "Jeremy, this ride is getting rough."

"It sure is," agreed Basil, "it's beginning to rain again too." The rain came pouring down harder than before.

"I think the river is getting wider," Jeremy shouted over the sound of the rain. "I can hardly see the sides."

The wind blew and the little raft twisted and turned. It moved faster and faster in the pouring rain.

The tiny creatures clung to their raft as it bobbed up and down on the water.

"Don't be afraid," said Jeremy, who was really a little afraid himself. We have to have faith like Noah did. We'll be all right. This river has to end somewhere."

Just then — BUMP! — the little raft stopped, blocked by some rocks in the middle of the stream. The clouds parted and the rain stopped as quickly as it had begun. The three friends looked around them.

"Wow!" said Basil. "That was some ride!"

"It sure was," said Jennie. "I wonder where we are."

They climbed off the raft onto one of the rocks. "This is just like what happened in the story of Noah," said Jeremy.

"What happened to Noah after the rain stopped?" asked Jennie.

"Well, the ark landed on a mountain top. Noah looked out the window, but he didn't know where they were. He sent out a raven and a dove, but they came back because the trees were still covered by water and there was no place for them to land.

"Noah waited another seven days. Then he sent the dove out again. This time she came back carrying an olive branch. And Noah knew the water was drying up and uncovering the land.

"When the water went down, God opened the door of the
ark. Outside the grass was green and things were growing. The
animals hurried out of the ark and down the mountainside.
Noah and his family came out and thanked God for keeping
them safe.

"Then God promised Noah that he would never again flood
the earth. God created the very first rainbow in the sky as a
sign that he would keep that promise forever."

"Well," said Jennie. "I'm not a dove, but I can fly. Maybe I can find out where we are."

"That's a great idea," said Jeremy. "Instead of an olive branch, maybe you can find a path home."

"Or maybe even our parents," added Basil hopefully. They were beginning to feel a little better now.

"I'm on my way," Jennie called, and off she flew.
  While Basil and Jeremy waited, they ate some of the snacks and talked about Noah's adventure and their own.

It wasn't long before Jennie was back. "We're safe!" she cried. "They're coming for us — our parents and friends. They began looking for us as soon as the rain started again."

The three friends said a quiet prayer of thanks. Overhead
the sky filled with colors, and a beautiful rainbow appeared —
a sign of God's promise to Noah and of his love for the world.